T5-COB-985
HARRIS COUNTY PUBLIC LIBRARY

Western Shambl W-SS
Shambley, Timothy
Slade River

MAY 18 2017 $15.99
            ocn960293319

Slade River

Slade River

Timothy Shambley

Copyright © 2016 by Timothy Shambley.

Library of Congress Control Number:		2016916209
ISBN:	Hardcover	978-1-5245-4635-9
	Softcover	978-1-5245-4634-2
	eBook	978-1-5245-4633-5

All rights reserved. No part of this book may be reproduced or transmitted in any form or by any means, electronic or mechanical, including photocopying, recording, or by any information storage and retrieval system, without permission in writing from the copyright owner.

This is a work of fiction. Names, characters, places and incidents either are the product of the author's imagination or are used fictitiously, and any resemblance to any actual persons, living or dead, events, or locales is entirely coincidental.

Any people depicted in stock imagery provided by Thinkstock are models, and such images are being used for illustrative purposes only.
Certain stock imagery © Thinkstock.

Print information available on the last page.

Rev. date: 09/28/2016

To order additional copies of this book, contact:
Xlibris
1-888-795-4274
www.Xlibris.com
Orders@Xlibris.com
736644

Contents

Partners 1

Rustlers 13

Payday 37

Lost 57

Friends in Need 79

PARTNERS

Chapter 1

The weather was changing; it was getting colder up here, high in the mountains. The snow could be coming within the next ten to fifteen days. And if a man got caught up here in the snow, it would take three months or more before he could get back down to the lower elevation. As he sat by his campfire, he thought about that. He was also thinking how long he had been gone from his wife and son already. He would give it two more days, and then he would start back home. Two more days. He had already been on the trail for almost three weeks, and he was no closer to finding his objective than he was the morning he left town.

He could still remember that morning. He was just sitting down to breakfast with Sarah and Billy when he heard a rider coming up to the front yard at a gallop. He got up from the table and went out the front door. It was John Parker. John dismounted, letting the reins from his horse trail on the ground.

"What's your hurry this morning, John?"

"Sheriff, we just had a shooting in town."

"Who got shot?" asked Sarah, peering out the door.

As John came up on the porch, they could see for the first time how shaken he was.

"It was Mr. Bailey. He was coming up the street to open up this morning, and as he turned the corner by the saloon, Navajo Joe came out and pulled his gun and shot him. No warning! Nothing! Just pulled his gun and shot!"

That had happened about three weeks ago. When Mike left his house, he had told Sarah to pack enough supplies for two weeks. He knew that trailing Navajo Joe was going to be tough, if not impossible. Now as he sat drinking his coffee, he was getting the feeling that it was impossible. All Mike knew about the shooting was what John and the saloonkeeper had told him. They were the only people in town that saw what happened. The story was that Navajo Joe had gone to Mr. Bailey's store the day before the shooting and wanted to buy some supplies on credit. Navajo Joe got mad and told him he would get his supplies or someone would be sorry. Mr. Bailey still refused him the supplies, and Joe left. Then the shooting happened the next morning. It was plain and simple murder.

Mike got up, banked his fire for the night, and was just spreading his groundsheet when he heard a horse.

"Hello, the fire! I'm friendly. Can I come up?"

Mike knew that voice; it was an old trapper by the name of Lucky Jack.

"Sure, Lucky, come on in."

When Lucky came in, his face broke into a grin. "Mike, what in thunder brings you way out here this time of year?"

As Mike poured the coffee and gave Lucky a plate of beans, he told him the story of Navajo Joe.

"That's a shame what happened to Mr. Bailey, Mike. But you can head back home, Joe's dead. He ran into some friends of mine a couple of days back. He thought he needed them furs worse than they did, but they kinda showed him different. He's buried about twelve miles east of here."

So that was the end of that. Mike would head back home. He should be able to make it in about three days.

Chapter 2

HOMECOMING

It was early in the afternoon when Mike rode down the street of his town. He had decided to come into town before he went home. There was the report on Navajo Joe to write, and he wanted to tell the widow Bailey that Navajo was dead. Jeff was seated behind his desk when Mike walked in. Jeff was a young cowhand that took over for Mike when he was away.

"How did the trip go, Mike?"

So Mike filled Jeff in on what had happened with Navajo Joe.

"Well, I guess that old Joe finally ran into somebody that wasn't afraid of him. And somebody that had a fair chance against him. Mike, why don't you head on home? You need rest, and I know that you want to see your family."

"You're right, Jeff. Sarah and the boy probably thought I dropped off the end of the world."

On the ride back to his ranch, Mike was thinking of the widow Bailey and what she would do without her husband. As Mike came around the bend of the trail, he thought he smelled smoke. Mike spurred his horse into a gallop. When he arrived at his ranch, his worst fears were confirmed. There in front of him lay the ashes of his home. Where were Sarah and his son?

He jumped down from his horse and ran into the yard, screaming their names. As he got to the ashes, he found Sarah. There was no helping her. Next thing was to find his son. About one hundred feet away, near the remains of the barn, he found his son. The boy had been beaten to death.

Mike fell to his knees and began sobbing. Why did this have to happen? What did these two innocent people do to deserve this?

After burying his family, Mike started to look around for clues. He knew this wasn't the work of Indians because none of his stock had been run off. And Sarah had been violated. No matter what people thought of the Indians, they would never violate a woman. And they would also have taken the horses.

After searching around the place for an hour or more, he knew who the killers were. He remembered the case. How long had it been? Six or seven years? The Claytons, Brad and Tooley—two brothers that tried to rob a stage in these parts. Mike trailed them and arrested them. At the trial, the judge gave them ten years. After the sentencing, Tooley looked right at Mike and swore to everyone that the sheriff would pay for what he had done to them.

There it was, scratched on a rock by where his son had been—the name *Tooley*.

"Well, Tooley, looks like you made good on your promise. But now, instead of a woman and a boy, you're going to have to deal with me!" Mike sat on his horse and looked down at where his ranch used to be. Knowing what he was about to do would change his life forever did not alter his resolve to avenge the deaths of his loved ones.

Chapter 3

THE HUNT

It had been a month since Mike had buried his family. He had come up to this line cabin the day after the killings. He needed to get away to think and plan his strategy. Now that he had this part done, it was time to start the hunt. He went to the corral and talked to his horse.

"It's going to be a hard road, boy. We may not come out of this alive, but we won't be the only ones."

He was thinking that he was going to go west toward Pine Ridge. Pine Ridge was a known hangout for the rough element, and it lay about twenty miles west of where he was now. He went back into the cabin and picked up his saddle and bedroll. Then he got his coat, put it on, and left.

It was late when he walked his horse up to the doors at the stable. Only after a careful look around did he dismount and put his horse up in one of the stalls. After he rubbed the horse down and fed it some corn, he picked up his saddlebags and Winchester and walked toward the door.

"Nice night out there. Be careful. We have some pretty rough boys in town."

Mike turned his head and saw the holster standing in the doorway of the tack room.

"Yeah, it is a nice night. But the guys I'm looking for aren't too tough—they just kill women and children." Then he walked out the door.

The holster turned his head and spoke over his shoulder. "I don't know who he is hunting, boy, but I'll tell you one thing. I'm glad it's not me."

"Who was it, Pa?"

"Son, his name is Mike Rivers. Last I heard, he was sheriff of a little town called Applegate. But before that, he was a bounty hunter who collected on every bounty he went after."

Mike walked into the saloon and looked around. There were six men at the bar, and there was a game of poker going at one of the tables. It was like any other saloon that Mike had been in, but there was one big difference. There, at the bar, stood the Clayton brothers. Finally, the hunt was over. Mike thought about what he should do. The saloon was too crowded to start anything. He also had no idea how many friends the Claytons had in town, not to mention right here in the saloon.

Chapter 4

THE PLAN

One thing that Mike had going for him was that the Claytons hadn't noticed him. Mike slipped out the back door of the saloon into the dark alley. He stood there for a few minutes, letting his eyes grow accustomed to the dark. Then he walked down to the corner. Looking around the street, he saw the diner was still open. Mike opened the door, walked in, and sat down where he could keep his eye on the saloon across the street.

He was sitting over his third cup of coffee when a tall man walked in and sat down next to him.

"How's the food here?"

"It beats cooking your own over an open fire," Mike replied.

"I sure hope so. I've been eating my own cooking for so long that I'm just about starved. You're kinda a long way from Applegate, ain't ya?"

Mike looked up from his plate and stared at the man, trying to place the face.

"You're one up on me, stranger. You seem to know me, but I sure can't place your face."

"My name's Tom Slade. And if the holster at the stable is right, you'd be Mike Rivers, sheriff from over at Applegate."

"You sure got the name right, mister, but I ain't the sheriff no more."

Tom looked at Mike. He was getting ready to ask what had happened when, all of a sudden, Mike got up and went out the door. The Claytons were at the hitching rail, tightening the cinches on their horses. Mike opened the door and stepped out on the boardwalk.

"Tooley Clayton, can I have a word with you?"

The Claytons turned around to see who was calling them, but all they could see was a dark form beside the building.

"Yeah, sure. You want to talk, you just come over here, and we will have us a nice little talk."

"Brad, you stay out of this! I've got a Winchester right on your belt buckle!"

That was Tom at the door, but what did he want out of this? Mike didn't ask Tom to get involved, but he sure wasn't going to turn down the help either. Mike stepped into the street, and right beside him was Tom.

"Brad! I'm Tom Slade of the Texas Rangers. You and Tooley are under arrest! Just drop your guns right where you are!"

The Claytons dropped their hardware in the street and stood there waiting.

"Tom, I don't know what you want them for, but these two murdered my family about two months ago. And I'm going to kill both of them!"

"No, Mike, I can't let you do that. I've got a warrant for these men signed by the governor of Texas for escaping."

Mike looked at the Claytons and all the hate just left him.

"Well, Tom, I guess you're right. But I want to tack murder charges onto that warrant."

The Claytons just laughed and said, "You can't prove it was us who beat your boy."

"Well, Tooley, I don't think he has to. You just confessed."

And with that, Tom grabbed Tooley. And with Mike behind Brad, with his gun on him, they walked to the jail.

With the Claytons in the jail, Mike and Tom went back to the diner to drink coffee and to finish their meal.

"Mike, I know that this wasn't the way you wanted it to end. But it's the best way, and you know it. This way, you are still on the side of the law and not a murderer like the Claytons. I'm looking for a new partner, and the major of my outfit said I could hire who I wanted, and he would stand by it. Mike, I want you."

Mike sat silently for a few minutes. Finally, he said, "Well, Tom, this chapter of my life is at an end. So yeah, I'll be your partner."

And that was how their partnership started.

RUSTLERS

Chapter 1

They pulled into a little cow town in Texas one evening and bedded the cattle down in a coral just outside of town. The trail boss had paid a couple of local cowboys to watch the herd so that his boys could go into town. The two cowhands and their dog, Sam, went to the barbershop. They received shaves and haircuts while Sam just lay on the boardwalk, watching people go by. Next, the two cowhands went to the diner and had something to eat and a pot of coffee.
"You guys come in with that herd out there?"

The cowhands looked up to see a young boy, about eleven years old, standing at their table.

"Yes we did, son."

"Well, all I have to say is you are a bunch of cattle thieves!" replied the boy. And after saying that, he ran out the door.

Well, the cowhands just sat there looking at each other.

Then one of them called the waitress over. "Miss, do you know who that boy that was just in here was?"

After looking around the room, she looked him right in the eye. "Yes, I do. That was Jimmy Smithers. You should know. You're holding his grandfather's cattle just outside of town!"

"Now wait a minute," replied one of the cowhands. "We just hired someone back down the trail. If those are his cattle, why doesn't anyone go to the law?"

About that time, the door opened, and three cowboys that got hired before Mike and Tom walked in.

"Hey, you! Your fleabag dog just bit me. I think I'll have to skin him for it."

"Well, friend—and I use the term loosely—my dog couldn't have bitten you. See, he is still out there and very much alive. As for skinning him . . . Well, quite frankly, you will have to go through me first. And I don't think you want to do that."

And at that, he pushed the empty chair beside him out of the way and dived headfirst at the man. When the man got up, Tom caught him with a right to the windpipe and a left to the mouth, splitting both lips so blood started pouring down the big man's mouth. When Lucas regained his composure, he came back like a bull in a china closet.

They stood in the middle of the diner toe-to-toe, slugging it out. Tom got hit so hard that he could have sworn Lucas had axe handles swinging instead of fists. Blood was running down his face and getting into his eyes. Finally, Tom saw his opening as Lucas dropped his right, just for a split second. Then Tom stepped in and started pounding—rights to the head and lefts to the body. Finally, after a right to the head followed by a left to the chin, Lucas lay on the floor. He was out cold.

Before Tom could get his head clear, he heard a scream and growling and snarling. He turned around to see Sam on top of the other cowboy with his gun hand in his mouth. "Sam! Let go! Now, friend, that was really stupid," he said to the man. "I could kill you for that, and I have enough witnesses here that saw you try to shoot me in the back."

About that time, the sheriff walked in and asked, "What happened here?"

Before Tom could say anything, Lucas said, "Just a little misunderstanding, Sheriff." Tom was standing there, kind of dumbfounded. He just couldn't believe that the sheriff didn't ask any more questions or that no one else would speak up. He did notice though that the man Sam had attacked and the other cowboy had moved around the room. One was behind the waitress, and one was behind his partner, Mike. And he would be willing to bet they were both covered with guns.

After the sheriff left, Lucas and his man started for the door. But before he left, he said, "Next time we meet, you may not be so lucky."

Before he got to the door, Tom said, "Lucas, there's one thing I need to know. What do you have hanging over this town's head?"

Chapter 2

When Tom and Mike got back to the corral the next morning, the herd seemed to be a little thinner than it was the night before.

"Mike, I just don't know what to make of this situation. I think that I'm going to ride down to the diner and get some breakfast. You going to come along?"

"No, Tom. I think me and Sam should check out some of the other places in town."

When Tom walked into the diner, the only ones there were Jimmy Smithers, the cook, and the waitress.

"Hi, Jimmy. Do you mind if I sit down and have a man-to-man talk with you?"

"Do what you want to," said Jimmy.

"Jimmy, the other day, you told my partner and me that those cattle were your grandfather's. Now I'm not calling you a liar—but, son, there were no brands on these cattle. They were all mavericks."

"Yes, sir, that's right," said Jimmy. "They were all mavericks. My grandfather, Pa, and me spent most of the spring bringing them cows out of the hills. We had us almost four hundred head rounded up at our place, ready to brand."

"Can I get you gentlemen something to eat?"

Tom looked up, and for the first time, he noticed the waitress. She was about five feet four inches tall with brown hair and big brown eyes.

Jimmy said, "Kathy, this is . . . I'm sorry. I didn't ask you your name."

"My name is Tom, Jimmy. It is nice to meet both of you. And yes, Kathy, we will take whatever you have to eat. I'll have coffee, please. And give my friend here some milk."

Mike was sitting at a table in the saloon a couple of buildings down from the diner. He was drinking a beer. It was a little early for him, but after fifteen years of this type of work, he had been through this sort of thing before. There was no better place for information than saloons and diners. And long ago in their partnership, it was decided by Mike that he would take the saloons, and Tom could have the diners. Mike liked it that way because he got along better with the rougher element.

The barkeep came to Mike's table with a fresh beer. "Did you ride in with the herd the other day?"

"Yeah," Mike replied.

"Well then, I guess you probably expect to run a tab until the trail boss decides to move on."

"What?" replied Mike. "Is that the way you usually do business?"

The barkeep said, "Well, sir, since it's just you and me in here right now—no, it ain't.

But when Bricker's outfit comes into town, that's the way it is done. And then when they do leave, you might get paid—but most likely not!"

"Thanks for the beer. How much do I owe you?"

After Mike paid, he went down the street to the general store. He needed some new shirts and pants, and he wanted to look around.

After they had finished eating, Tom sat back with another cup of coffee.

"Well, Jimmy, you want to finish telling me about your grandfather?"

"Like I was telling you, we had just about four hundred head of mixed mavericks. Well, we was going to start branding, then Pa had an accident."

Tom asked, "What kind of accident?"

"Well," said Jimmy, "he had come into town to file for a brand. While he was here, Bricker said that he was missing some cattle from his driving herd. Next thing that Grandpa and me heard, Pa had been shot."

Tom asked, "You mean Bricker shot him?"

"No, sir. Bricker don't do any of his shooting. He has it done for him."

"Did you go to the sheriff?" asked Tom.

"Are you kidding? He was there! Sheriff Duncan is as afraid of Bricker as the rest of the town. Besides that, he's the one that gave them the cows."

"What about your grandpa? Can't he do anything about it?"

"No," said Jimmy. "He's been out at the ranch sick, and Bricker has a couple of men out there making sure no one causes trouble."

"Aren't you afraid that they will hurt you or your grandfather?"

"Well, yes, sir. I am a little, but they killed my pa and stole my ranch and cattle. Sir, my pa's dead, my grandpa's sick, and if I want to get what's rightfully mine, it's up to me to get it."

After Jimmy got up and left, Kathy came over with the coffeepot and sat down. "Did you and Jimmy have a nice chat?"

"Yes, we did. He is a very strong young man. I understand that his father was killed here in town."

"Yes, he was. Now if you will excuse me."

As Kathy got up to leave, Tom couldn't help but notice that she was crying.

Mike came in and got a cup and poured himself some coffee. "Strange town here. Did you know that when you ride for Bricker, you work for free?"

Chapter 3

"What are you talking about, Mike?"

Mike told Tom what went on in the saloon and the conversation that he had with the barkeep.

"Then I went to the store to get some shirts, jeans, underwear, and a couple of boxes of .44s. Well, I walked in there and placed my order, and while the storekeeper was filling it, three hombres walked in behind me. One was the one Sam tangled with last night.

"Well, when the storekeeper turned back around, he was white as a ghost! I knew the guys were behind me and figured that they were spoilin' for a fight. Funny thing was, Sam wasn't growling. So I went to pay the man, and he said my money ain't no good here and to just take it and have a nice day.

"Now, Tom, I ain't never stole anything in my life, and I told him that. So I just left the stuff on the counter. Tom, what's going on here?"

"I don't know, Mike. I just don't know."

Tom then told Mike about the talk he had with Jimmy.

"That's kinda interesting, Tom, but there ain't no four hundred head of cattle out in the corral."

"I know, Mike. So they must have another holding ground for them somewhere. What do you say we go back to the store and see about getting our supplies?"

When they walked into the store, the storekeeper froze in his tracks when he saw Mike.

"Hi, mister, do you remember me?"

"Yeah, what do you two gentlemen want?"

"My friend told me he was in here this morning to buy supplies, and he had a problem paying for them."

"No, sir. You two work for Bricker, don't you?"

"Yes, mister. By the way, what is your name?"

"My name's Potter."

"Well, Mr. Potter, why wouldn't you take my friend's money?"

"I told you that if you work for Bricker, your money is no good."

"Now that's what my friend tried to tell me, but I just don't understand it. So why don't you try to explain it to both of us?"

"You guys really don't understand, do you? Bricker runs this country and does whatever he wants."

"Why hasn't anyone gone to the law about it? It seems that you have a sheriff right here in town."

"You must not hear good, mister. I said that Bricker owns this whole country. That includes the law."

"Well, I'll tell you what, Mr. Potter. My name is Tom, and this is my riding partner, Mike. And that there fleabag is Sam. And we may have ridden in with that herd, and it's beginning to look like a big mistake on our part. But we pay for our supplies, and nobody owns us—not even Bricker. So if you would be so kind to fill our orders, we will pay you and be on our way."

"Sir, it would be my pleasure. And, Mike, I'm sorry for the way that I acted earlier this morning."

While Potter was getting the orders filled, Mike and Tom went outside on the street and had a smoke.

"Well, Tom, that's one person that knows where we stand."

"No, Mike, that's three. The owner of the cattle, Jimmy Smithers. And I'm pretty sure Kathy knows where we stand."

When they got done with their smokes, they turned to go back inside and ran into Lucas and his three riders.

"Well, boys, look who it is—it's the mutt lovers. I told you that you may not be as lucky as you were the other night."

"Look, Lucas, I don't know what your problem is, but I whipped you fair the other night. And your man there got you off lucky because by rights, with him pulling a gun on a man, I could have shot him.

He's just lucky that my dog listens to me, or he would be worse off than just his arm in a sling."

"My arm may be in a sling, stranger, but I can still shoot your mutt!"

"Lucas, I don't know who that man is, but you might jog his memory about what happened to the last man that thought he was going to skin my dog."

"Haden, let it be! You couldn't whip this man with two good arms."

And with that, Lucas, Haden, and the other man stalked down the boardwalk toward the saloon. When Tom and Mike entered the store again, Mr. Potter had their packages put together.

"Well, Tom, I guess what you said is true. You sure don't belong to nobody but yourself," said the storekeeper.

"What are you talking about, Mr. Potter? We had a little run-in with them a couple of nights ago at the diner."

"You boys really do not know anything about Bricker, do you? That big fellow, Lucas, is his right-hand man. He is the one that comes into town with the herds, holds them here for three days, sometimes as long as a week, and then they just move on."

"Do they always hold them in the same pen right outside of town there?" Mike asked.

"Well, that's funny. Sometimes they come in with a fair-size herd of, say two hundred to three hundred head. But by the time they leave out there, there may be a hundred to a hundred and fifty head. And none of the cowboys ever seemed worried about it."

Mike and Tom looked at each other and frowned a little bit. Tom picked up the packages, and before they left, they said, "Thanks, Mr. Potter. And please remember what I said. We pay for our supplies. And if you would, could you keep this talk we just had between us?"

"Sure thing. And thanks again."

Chapter 4

When they got back to the hotel and went to their room to put their supplies away, Mike asked Tom about Jimmy.

"Well, we had breakfast this morning. And after talking to him, I get the feeling that he is on the up and up about owning those cows. The only thing I can't figure out is he said there are about four hundred head when you and I both know that when we started, there weren't anywhere near half that many. So where did the other two hundred head go?

"And another thing he said was that when his pa came into town to file a brand, he was shot. When I asked him who shot his pa, he said that he didn't know. But he did know it wasn't Bricker because he doesn't do any of his own killing."

Tom and Mike got cleaned up and went downstairs to the diner to eat. When they walked in, the first person they saw was Jimmy.

"Hi, Jimmy. Do you mind if my friend and I join you?"

"Huh? No, Tom. Go ahead."

"Jimmy Smithers, this is my riding partner, Mike."

"Yeah, nice to meet you, sir. Are you a square shooter like Tom?"

"Well, I like to think that I am, Jimmy. Tom and I have been riding together for a mighty long time now."

"Then I can talk in front of you just like I can with Tom?"

"Yes sir, Jimmy. If you want to, you can. But let's order something to eat first, OK?"

Kathy came over to their table and took their orders and left. Tom and Mike sat back with their coffee and listened as Jimmy talked about his ranch.

Tom asked, "How is your grandfather doing, Jimmy? Have you been home to see him?"

"No, sir. Every time I ride out to the ranch, one of Bricker's men comes out and tells me to go out and head back to town. Tom, I haven't seen my grandfather for two weeks now. I don't even know if he is still alive or not."

"Mike, what do you say you and me take a ride out to Jimmy's ranch tomorrow morning and check things out? Jimmy, if we can get your grandfather back to town, is there anybody here that can help you take care of him?"

"I will. You get Mr. Smithers back here, and Jimmy and I will take care of him."

It was Kathy who had spoken; she had just come to the table with their food. "Mister, if you two are serious about helping Jimmy and his grandfather, I'll be more than happy to help them out any way that I can when they get into town."

The following morning, Tom, Mike, and Sam hit the trail east out of town. It was about six miles to the Smithers ranch.

"You know, Mike, after looking at this range—the grass, the water holes, and the natural boundaries—I can see why Bricker is trying to keep Jimmy off. But why run the cattle off? It just doesn't figure."

"Yeah, I know what you mean, Tom. They've got the cattle. And evidently, they have control of the ranch. So why keep the old man around?"

As they rode on, they kept thinking the situation over in their minds. They rounded a bend, and the ranch lay out in front of them. There was a pole corral, a barn, and a nice-looking cabin.

"Well, Mike, one thing's for sure. This ain't no roughshod outfit that put this together." Tom noticed Sam's ears perk up, and he started to growl a little. "Easy, boy. We got us one to the right of the woodpile."

"I got him spotted, Tom. I also got one in the hayloft. They ain't real friendly, are they?"

"No, Mike, they're not. Jimmy said that there were only three, and I'll bet the other one is in the house."

"Hello!" Tom yelled in the direction of the house.

The door opened, and a man in his late sixties walked out on the porch. "Can I help you boys?"

"We were just riding through," replied Tom, "and were hoping maybe you might have some coffee on and some range news or just any kind of talk."

This had to be Grandpa Smithers. The odd thing was he didn't look sick to Tom.

"Sure thing! Tie your horses up and come on in."

Tom and Mike tied their horses at the water trough and loosened the cinches on their saddles. Remembering the two men hiding in the yard, they took their Winchesters out of their scabbards and went on into the cabin.

"Sit down, boys. I was just making myself something to eat."

"That sounds good," Tom said.

"How far have you boys come?"

Mike turned around from the front door and looked at Tom and waited for him to answer.

"We came from around El Paso—just riding around, seeing new country. Quite a spread you have here. Do you plan to run any cattle on it?"

The old man looked up from his cooking and said, "I haven't thought of it. It's just me out here by myself now that my son has passed away. And I was just sort of thinking of living the rest of my time out here peacefully."

The old man put the plates and cups on the table. He dished up bacon, beans, doughnuts, and fresh black coffee. The food was really good.

"I haven't had beans this good since I was a little boy back in Fort Worth," Mike said.

"Thank you. My wife taught me how to bake them many years ago, and I guess every time I make them, it makes me feel like she and my son are still around."

"I'll bet Jimmy likes them too, doesn't he?" Tom asked.

The old man turned around with fire in his eyes. "What do you know about Jimmy? If you've done anything to him, I'll kill both of you!"

Tom looked at Mike and then back at the old man. "Now hold on there, Jimmy is fine. He's in town at the hotel, staying with that waitress, Kathy. My name is Tom, and this is my riding partner, Mike. And I'm going to guess that you are Jimmy's grandfather, Mr. Smithers, right?"

"Yeah, but that still doesn't explain what you're doing here. And what do you know about Jimmy?"

"The only thing that I know right now is what he has told me—about his ranch, a dead pa that the town sheriff won't do anything about, and a sick grandfather that he is worried about. Well, two factors add up. But, mister, you sure don't look sick to me." Tom had purposefully left the part about the cattle out because there was something wrong here, and he wasn't sure just yet what it was.

"Well, you tell Jimmy I'm all right. Don't worry about me and just stay in town with Kathy. And when I think it's time for him to come home, I'll come into town and get him."

"I'll do that. And thanks for the grub and coffee."

When Tom and Mike were outside, mounting up to ride away, Mike asked Tom if he thought the old man seemed to be acting a little funny.

"Yeah, Mike, I thought he was acting a little funny too. I mean he said he lived alone, but did you notice he had enough grub cooked up for four or five men? And another thing. Did you happen to notice he kept looking at that inside door like there was something or someone behind it?"

Mike sat on his horse, rolling a smoke and thinking. Jimmy had told Tom that there were usually three men out here with his grandfather. Now when they rode up, they spotted two of them outside. One was in the hayloft, and one was behind the woodpile. So where did that leave the third man?

"You know, Tom, you might have something there. I mean about somebody being in that other room. You remember Jimmy said that there were always at least three out here. And when we rode up, we only spotted two."

On the ride back to town, Tom couldn't help but wonder about the day's events and the way that old man Smithers had acted. The man told him and Mike that he did not plan on running any cattle on his land. Yet Mike and he both knew that he had cattle stolen from him, and at least some of them were sitting right outside of town. And another thing, he didn't want to go into details about his life. He told them that he lived alone, that his son had died, and that he wanted them to believe that was the only family he had. But when Tom mentioned Jimmy, the old man became real defensive.

When they got back to town, they went to the hotel. They went to their room, cleaned up, and went back down to the diner.

Chapter 5

Lucas, Haden, and their other friend were sitting at a table in the saloon when another man walked in and sat down with them.

"Had us some visitors out to the ranch today—a couple of hombres with a dog."

Lucas looked at him and then at the other two at the table. "What did they want out there?" he asked.

"I don't know. They went inside with the old man, ate with him, and just talked about range conditions. Oh, there was one other thing. They told him that girl from the diner is taking care of his grandson for him."

When the man got up and left, Lucas ordered the table another beer and looked over at the other two guys and said, "Boys, I don't like this. Nobody is supposed to be out at that ranch, especially talking to that old man. Haden, you keep an eye on that kid and girl, and me and Dan will watch those two riders for a while."

Kathy and Jimmy were at the store visiting with Mr. Potter while Mr. Potter was filling Kathy's order. The door opened, and Haden walked in and kind of hung around the dry goods, watching.

He looked at Jimmy and said, "Hey, boy, how's your granddaddy doing? Hear he's been feeling poorly?"

Jimmy didn't say anything to him; he just ignored him and stood a little closer to Kathy. Haden came up a little closer to them.

"Boy, I'm talking to you, and I want an answer!" And with that, he slapped Jimmy across the mouth.

Kathy pulled Jimmy aside and stepped between them.

"Now that you have hit a little boy, do you want to hit a woman too?"

"No, lady, but I'm going to teach this kid some manners."

And with that, Haden pushed her out of the way, pulled his gun on Mr. Potter, and dragged Jimmy out of the store into the street. Haden beat Jimmy up pretty good in the street that day.

When he got done, he said, "You tell your friends to stay away from the ranch."

Tom and Mike went down for supper that evening. They were looking for Jimmy to tell him about his grandfather, but he wasn't in the diner. Kathy came to their table with the pot and cups. When they asked about Jimmy, she told them what had happened earlier that day at the store.

"You tell Jimmy that I will be by to see him later. Right now, I want to go see if Haden can do that to a man rather than a boy." After saying that, Mike slammed his cup down and walked out the door.

"Tom, don't you think you should go help him? I mean, there are three of them, and I've seen them before. It won't be one on one."

"Kathy, I'm going to tell you a story about Mike. You may have noticed that we ride together, but did you ever notice that when it comes to talking to people like you and Jimmy that I do most of that?"

"Yes, Tom, but what does that have to do with anything?"

"Well, you see, we've been riding together for about fifteen years now. And when you ride with someone for that long of a time, you get to know a lot about each other. About sixteen years ago, Mike's wife and son were killed. At the time, Mike was the town sheriff of Applegate. Mike had been hunting a man up in the hills. When he came back home, he found his family murdered. His wife had been assaulted and shot, and his son—who was not much older than Jimmy—had been beaten to death.

"Well, Mike found the two men who did it, and that's when we met and formed our partnership. One of these days, he will have had enough riding, and him and Sam will settle down somewhere."

"But I thought Sam was your dog. I mean, the other night in here when you had the fight with Lucas, he listened to you so well."

"Oh, that. Sam listens to both of us. Yeah, I guess he kinda started out being my dog, but he really takes up to Mike. Those two are a lot alike. Nice and gentle, but they will bite."

Tom told Kathy about their strange meeting with old man Smithers the previous day.

"That just doesn't sound like Joe. You mean he didn't mention anything about Jimmy?"

"No. And when we mentioned the good range that he had, he said he never intended to run any cattle on it either."

"Tom, there is something really wrong because that's all Joe and Jimmy ever talked about when they would come in here. They were always talking about the brand that they wanted. Because Jimmy used to say that Joe had checked brand books, and there was no way anybody could alter that brand with a running iron or a cinch ring."

"Now that's pretty interesting, Kathy. Have you seen this brand? Do you think you could draw it for me?"

"No, Tom, I haven't seen it. But I'll bet Jimmy would draw it for you if you asked him to. I'm getting ready to take his supper up to him. If you want, you could come with me. I'm sure he would be happy to see you."

Mike walked into the saloon. As usual, it was full for a Friday night. There were a couple of tables of poker going on, and one of the saloon girls was singing a song off-key about a cowboy that had lost his girl.

He made his way up to the bar and ordered a beer and just stood back and looked around. How many places like this had he been in during his lifetime? Same old crowd. Gamblers that never drank enough to dull their senses. Yet always aware that there were men there that drank enough. Who thought they could beat them at their game. Then there were the saloon girls, always there to make a cowboy feel special as long as that cowboy had money in his jeans and who would buy her drinks all night. Then there was the town drunk who sat off by himself, drinking to try and forget whatever his life's problems were.

As he thought about all these people, he also began to think about himself. Maybe that's why he didn't mind doing this part of the work and letting Tom have the other part. Because the more he thought about it, all these people were just like him in a way. They were all searching for something in their lives. And yes, he had to admit it; they were probably lonely like him.

"Do you want another beer, friend?"

It was the bartender.

"Yeah, sure. Hey, I'm looking for somebody. Maybe you can help me."

Mike made sure that he raised his voice just a little bit for the next part.

"Earlier today, two friends of mine were over at Mr. Potter's store doing some shopping. Some of you might know them—Miss Kathy from the diner and Jimmy Smithers, an eleven-year-old boy."

A hush fell over the room, so Mike lowered his voice to a conversational tone.

"Well, it seems that while my friends were shopping, this fellow named Haden came in and started proddin' little Jimmy, asking about his grandfather or something. Well, anyways, that don't matter. What matters is what this Haden fellow did to little Jimmy. It seems he took this eleven-year-old boy out in the street and beat him. Yeah, I guess he had to show him what kind of man he was. Well, folks, I'm here to tell you right now that I don't take to that. I don't see him in here or any of the crowd he runs with either. But if any of you know him or see him, tell him I'm looking for him. Or if he wants to find me, I'm staying at the hotel."

After Mike had left, one of the customers looked at the bartender and said, "That guy was just lucky that Haden or any of his bunch weren't here tonight."

The bartender looked back at the guy with cold eyes and a little smile.

"No, I think that maybe Hayden and them boys just bit off more than they can chew. I think I know that man from somewhere. And if it's who I'm thinking it is, Haden better leave the country."

After Jimmy had finished his supper, Kathy took the dishes downstairs.

"Thanks for coming and seeing me, Tom. But where's Mike? I was hoping he'd be with you."

"He's going to come up and see you later, Jimmy. He had him some business he wanted to get done."

He continued, "Jimmy, we saw your grandfather the other day, but something didn't seem right. You told me he was sick. The man we talked to wasn't sick. And he didn't seem to know anything much about the ranch, much less you."

"Tom, what did this man look like?"

"He was about six feet, has gray hair, stooped shoulders, and brown eyes."

"You know why he didn't know anything? You just described Bricker! My grandfather is six feet four inches, has gray hair, blue eyes, and walks with a limp."

The door opened and Kathy walked in, followed by Mike and Sam.

"I thought you men might like the last of the peach pie that we had. And I even have a bone for you, Sam."

Tom told Mike about their meeting with Bricker.

"Well, no wonder that man seemed so out of place there. Jimmy, that room off the kitchen—is that a bedroom? And does it have a window with a way to get around to it without being seen?"

"Yeah, it does. Why?"

"You just let me worry about that and you get yourself better. By the way, don't worry about Haden no more. The whole town knows what he did, and he's looking for me now."

After they finished the pie and were getting ready to leave, Tom said, "Oh yeah, I almost forgot what I really came up here for. Kathy was telling me about this brand of yours that nobody can use a running iron or a cinch ring on."

"Yeah, it's a good one. Grandpa spent almost a year on it. Then we went and checked to make sure nobody else had filed for it before we did."

"But I thought you never got it filed. I thought that's why they shot your pa," Mike said.

"Yes, sir, they shot Pa all right. But we already had the brand filed. He was just coming to town to get another iron made. And when Grandpa is safe here in town and I'm back on my feet—you know the other two hundred or so head of cattle out of my herd that aren't here in town? Well, I know where they are, and I'm taking them back to my ranch!"

Chapter 6

As Tom, Mike, and Kathy left Jimmy's room, Tom said, "Now that was sure an interesting conversation. Mike, why don't we see if we can find out what became of that iron Jimmy's pa was having made?"

The next morning, while Mike and Tom were having breakfast, Lucas walked in and came over to their table.

"Here's your pay. Now you boys are free to leave anytime you want to, and I'm telling you to be out of town before tomorrow."

Tom said, "Now hold on there, Lucas. We'll take your money because I've heard that sometimes you have a little trouble paying your debts, but we will leave town when we are good and ready. I don't know about my partner here, but I kinda like this town, and I figure on staying on for a while."

"Suit yourselves, but you've been told."

"Hey, Lucas," said Mike, "you tell that skunk Haden that I'm going to find him. And when I do, he will wish he had never laid a hand on Jimmy Smithers."

When they had finished eating, they took Jimmy's breakfast up to him and asked him how he was feeling.

"I'm ready to go. Kathy said I need some fresh air, so I'm going."

"Hold on, Jimmy. You just give me and Mike one more day. OK?"

"No, sir! I can't! I heard Lucas say that they were going to move my cattle this morning, so I got to get them today."

Mike and Tom looked at each other and finally at Jimmy.

"Look, Jimmy," said Tom, "we're here to help you. But now is the time for us to be totally honest with you, OK? We are undercover Texas Rangers. We've been after Bricker for a long time. But we haven't been able to catch him with any branded cattle. So you see, Jimmy, we really need to catch him with some branded stuff to do any good."

"Is that all you guys need? Why didn't you say so? I have some branded stuff."

"Where, Jimmy?"

"Let's go! I'll show you!"

Mike, Jimmy, and Tom left east out of town. They had gone halfway to Jimmy's ranch when Jimmy took a little-used trail up the mountains to the south.

"This is where we brought them in for branding. It's a natural basin full of water, three walls, and that way, we only had to put that one pole gate up. Then we just left them here to fatten up."

It was about two hundred acres of rolling green hills, thick grass, and plenty of water.

"Tom, would you look at this? A body could ride right by here and never even know it."

"We did the other day. Remember, Mike?"

"Grandpa picked this place just for that reason. Well, anyway, there's the rest of my herd. All branded."

As Mike and Tom rode around the stock, they noticed the good condition that they were in and also the brand.

"You know, Mike, I've been studying that brand, and I've never seen it before either. And Jimmy's right. That would be awful hard to run an iron over."

They rode over to where Jimmy was sitting on his horse. Mike was the first one to speak.

"Jimmy, you have a fine-looking herd here. But Tom and I noticed when we were riding with the other herd that once in a while, it seemed to get a little thinner. So, son, I'm afraid it still might be short a few head."

"Well, I was wondering if anyone else was going to notice that. No, sir, I'm not short on any cows. You see that old mossy horn steer over there? Well, the other cows just follow him wherever he goes. So me and him just sort of thinned the herd a couple of times."

Mike and Tom looked at Jimmy and then at each other and began to laugh.

"What are you guys laughing at?"

"Well, Jimmy, I've been kinda getting tired of Mike's company once in a while. Can you cook? Because if you can and you were about seven years older, I would trade you for Mike in a heartbeat."

Jimmy kinda smiled; it really made him feel good to be fussed over by these two. Since his pa had been killed, he had been kinda lonely, and these two men had helped fill the void that was left.

Mike and Tom were talking when they heard horse hooves approaching. They grabbed Jimmy's bridle, and all three rode for cover. When they were all safely hidden in the trees, they saw four men ride up to the gate.

"Here they are, boss. We finally found them. It took us forever, but we found them. Now if we can get rid of the old man, we have us a natural hideout for any other herds that we steal."

"Yes, it's perfect. No wonder that old man is so stubborn and won't sign the deed. Well, we got the son, and his ranch hand is as good as ours. Now we have all his cattle. All we need to do now is get that grandson of his."

"Don't you remember that Haden tried that and it didn't work? Remember, Bricker, that kid made him a couple of friends in those two cowboys."

Just then, Mike and Tom came out of their cover with their Winchesters drawn. "Bricker! Texas Rangers! Drop your weapons. You're under arrest for rustling, kidnapping, and brand altering."

Bricker went for his gun, as did the other three riders with him. In a matter of seconds, saddles were emptied.

Mike looked around and frowned then rode toward the gate.

Jimmy rode out. "Man, I've never seen anything like that. That was really something."

Tom looked at Jimmy and stopped their horses. "Now you listen to me, son. What you just saw was nothing but senseless killing. There was nothing neat or fast or good about it. Men died here. Granted, they may not have been good men, but they were still men. It could have just as easily been me and Mike or you with a stray bullet. Do you understand what I'm trying to say, Jimmy?"

"Yes, sir, I do."

"Good. Now let's catch up with Mike and go see your grandfather."

When Tom and Jimmy made it to the ranch, Mike and Jimmy's grandfather were on the porch, talking.

"Tom, I would like you to meet Mr. Smithers. We have been having a pretty interesting conversation. It seems that what little Jimmy said is right. But he didn't tell us one important thing, and this is pretty good. It seems that while Jimmy was thinning the herd in town and bringing them out here to the basin, he has been branding them himself. That's why we couldn't find the branding iron that Jimmy's pa had fixed."

"Well, imagine that, Mike. I think that we have us another ranger among us."

"Did you hear that, Grandpa? They just made me a Texas Ranger!"

"I sure did, Jimmy. I sure did."

Mike swung onto the saddle and said, "What do you say we go to town and help this cowboy bring his herd home, Tom?"

And with that, Mike and Tom—with Jimmy and Sam in the lead—headed toward town.

PAYDAY

Chapter 1

Mike and Tom were sitting in Major Clark's office.

"I wonder what the major wants us for. I've been working for him for five years now, and this is the first time he has sent for me when I was supposed to be off."

That was Tom talking; Mike knew that it must be something important. He and Tom had only been together for about a year now, and he really enjoyed it. But he had never seen his partner so nervous before.

The door to the office opened, and Major Clark entered the room. This was the first time that Mike had ever seen the major.

"Mike, it's nice to finally meet you. Tom has had nothing but good reports about you. I feel like I already know you."

"Thank you, Major. It's nice to meet you also. You must be a pretty good man yourself to put up with Tom for as long as you have."

"Now wait a minute, Mike. I don't think the major called for us just to listen to your big mouth."

Laughing, the major said, "You're right, Tom. The army sent me a message a couple of weeks ago and wants us to look into a problem for them."

"The army? Major, don't the army usually take care of their own problems?"

"Yes, Tom, they usually do. But Captain Tucker seems to think that it could be an inside job. That's where you and Mike come in. I know from your file that you were in the army once. And I also did some background checks on Mike—very impressive, by the way. But the thing that makes this job so right is that you were in the army also."

"Yes, sir, that's right. I was. But what's that got to do with this?"

"Well, since you asked. Gentlemen, I want you to meet your contact man while on this job."

The door opened, and in walked an army sergeant.

"Gentlemen, this is Sergeant Gibson from Fort Stanton. He will catch you up on the situation on your ride to the fort."

Mike, Tom, and Sergeant Gibson left the office and went across the street to the saloon. After the men ordered their drinks, Sergeant Gibson started filling Mike and Tom in on what had been happening.

"It all started about three months ago. We lost the first payroll about fifty miles from the fort. The stage left the bank in Marshall with three passengers. One was a teacher, and the other two were cattlemen. The army talked to all three of them, and the only thing that they could get was that there were four bandits, and one rode a big white stallion."

"What about the others? The major said that there were three all together. Did the army get any more clues from the other holdups?"

"No, Mike, we didn't learn anything else that was helpful. The only thing was that in all three, there was a man riding a big white stallion."

When the three men arrived at the fort, Mike and Tom knew all that Sergeant Gibson knew about the case. They learned from talking with Sergeant Gibson that aside from the fort commander and the payroll officer, the only other people who knew about when the payrolls were leaving the bank were the bank employees.

The three men went into Captain Tucker's tent to discuss what they planned on doing. Captain Tucker sat behind his desk, looking over some paperwork. He was a medium-built man of about forty years with salt-and-pepper hair—well, what was left of it. Captain Tucker looked up from his paperwork when they entered.

"Good morning, gentlemen. Please have a seat. I'll be with you in a minute. Sergeant Gibson, would you please leave us alone for a while?"

When the captain finished his paperwork, he reached for the coffeepot, which was on a potbellied stove behind his desk.

"Can I offer you men some coffee? It's not the best and probably not as strong as you're used to, but it is hot."

After the captain poured the coffee, he sat back behind his desk and lit up a pipe.

"I take it that Sergeant Gibson filled you in on the problem around here. You are probably wondering why the army has asked for your help and why we don't handle it ourselves. Well, I'll tell you two why you are here. I've known your Major Clark for a number of years now. We served together about twelve years ago. And I know the kind of man that he is and also the kind of men that work for him. And this job is tailored for him and the kind of men that you two must be."

Mike and Tom finished their coffee and looked at each other and then at the captain.

Tom was the first to speak. "Sir, you seem to know the major pretty well, but my partner and I still don't understand why the army wants Texas Rangers working on a case that is obviously an army matter."

"That's right, Captain," Mike concurred. "We all know the law. And in a matter such as this, the Texas Rangers have no jurisdiction."

The captain refilled their cups and sat back down.

"You're right, Mike, the Texas Rangers have no jurisdiction. But this paperwork in front of me gives you and Tom jurisdiction over this entire fort."

The captain handed the papers to Mike.

"Well, Tom, we are back in the army!"

Chapter 2

Mike and Tom had been at the fort for three days now, and their cover seemed to be working. The order that Captain Tucker had given them stated that they were both lieutenants in the army. The story that started around the fort was that the army was going to start a new post, and these lieutenants were here to see how one was run. This story worked well because that way, no one would get suspicious of them asking questions on how everything was run.

Mike was heading to the captain's tent when a young corporal approached him.

"Excuse me, Lieutenant, my name is Jones. Sergeant Gibson said that you wanted to talk to someone in dispatch?"

"That's right, Corporal. Are you in dispatch?"

"Yes, sir, I am. If you would, I can show you the office and any dispatches you would like to see."

"Thank you, Corporal. I would really like to see that."

Mike and Corporal Jones walked across the parade ground to the dispatch tent.

Tom was in Sergeant Gibson's tent, talking to him about the latest robbery.

"They struck last night the same way. No one hurt and a rider with a big white stallion. I don't know, Lieutenant, it just seems that it has to be an inside job."

"Well, Rod, it does sound like an inside job. But Mike and I haven't been able to put a loop around this one yet. We have talked to several different people, and we can't get a set pattern yet."

In the dispatch office, Mike was going through some old dispatches.

"Corporal, I've noticed that some of these dispatches were sent by a Corporal Pearson—and all of them around the same time that the stages were held up."

"Do you mind if I look at those, Lieutenant? I see what you mean. Would you like to talk to Corporal Pearson?"

"No. Not right now. Let's just keep this under wraps for a few days."

As Mike was leaving the dispatch tent, he ran into Tom in the street.

"Hi, Tom. Learn anything new?"

"No, just that they had another holdup last night. The same guy with the white stallion."

After Mike filled Tom in on his conversation and findings at the dispatch office, they both went to their tent to relax.

"Tom, I think that we should talk to this Corporal Pearson tomorrow."

"Yeah, Mike, you're right. And why don't we see if you can strike up a friendship with this Corporal Jones."

Chapter 3

The next morning, after they had breakfast, Mike got up and went to find Corporal Jones. Mike and Tom had talked about it the night before and had decided that Mike would use Corporal Jones to talk to Corporal Pearson. While Mike was doing this, Tom and Sergeant Gibson were going to payroll to talk to Sergeant Wilson.

When Tom and Sergeant Gibson walked into the payroll tent, they found Sergeant Wilson talking to another sergeant.

"I don't know what we are going to do. The men haven't been paid in over a month, and every time we think we are getting a payroll through, the same thing happens. Tell your men that we are trying everything, and as soon as we can, we will get them paid."

After the soldier left the tent, Sergeant Gibson introduced Tom to the payroll sergeant.

"Sergeant Wilson, I would like you to meet Lieutenant Slade. Him and Lieutenant Rivers are here for a couple of months to check us out."

"It's nice to meet you, sir. How can I help you?"

"Well, Sergeant, Lieutenant Rivers and I are going to start another fort, and we were sent here to see how this one is run."

"Well, Lieutenant, if you want to run a successful one, don't pattern your payroll office after this one."

"I've heard that you have had some trouble here. Can you explain any of it for me?"

"No, sir, I sure can't. I do know that it sure is hurting us pretty good. The men are getting pretty wild—what with no pay, they are pretty down in the dumps right now."

"I can understand that, but can't they get credit here at the post until they get paid?"

"Yes, sir, and that's one of the problems. You see, at most army posts, the army owns everything. But here at Stanton, we own everything but the dry goods store."

"What do you mean? How can the army not own the store?"

"Well, Lieutenant, when the army moved in here, the store was already here, so they just let the storekeeper stay. You see, this post is only a temporary post. So instead of upsetting the locals, they just let him stay."

"Well, that is strange. Do you know who authorized that? Was it someone from this post, or did it come from Washington?"

"I don't know, sir, but I think that it came from Washington."

"Thank you, Sergeant Wilson. We may be talking to you again."

Mike met with Tom at the saloon.

"Well, Tom, I talked to the payroll man, and he can't figure out what's going on either. He did tell us something interesting though."

"Yeah, what's that? I'm ready for some good news because I've hit nothing but dead ends."

"Well, it seems that the army owns everything here but the dry goods store. It appears that when the army moved in here, they let the storekeeper stay and run his business as usual."

"That is kind of strange. Have you talked to him yet?"

"No, I thought that maybe you could talk to him. I was going to send a wire to the major and let him know what's been going on. And while I'm there, I'm going to do some checking on those other wires that were sent."

"That sounds good. I'll head over to the store while you're doing that."

Chapter 4

Tom entered the store and took a look around. As he looked at all the supplies, he couldn't help but notice that it was pretty well stocked for a store at an army post.

"May I help you?"

Tom looked up to see a big man of about thirty-five or so. He didn't look like a typical storekeeper. He was about six feet four inches tall, solidly built, and weighed about 250 pounds. Tom was sure that this man was more comfortable in a saddle than he was behind the counter of a store.

"Yes, my name is Lt. Tom Slade. My friend Lieutenant Rivers and I just got to the post a couple of days ago, and we need to lay in some supplies."

"Well, Lieutenant, welcome to Fort Stanton. You've come to the right place. We have just about anything a body could want."

"I can see that. I couldn't help but notice that you're pretty well stocked for an army store."

"Yes, sir, I am. But the army doesn't tell me what to stock. I own this store, not the army."

"Yeah? That's what I hear. It seems funny to me that the army would let you do that."

"Well, it ain't that funny. I run my business, and the army runs theirs."

Tom could see that he wasn't going to get much information out of this man. He was already going on the defensive.

"Now just settle down here. I'm just here for some supplies. Here's my order. Would you please fill it?"

As the storekeeper was filling his order, Tom was looking at all the mining equipment on the shelves.

"Is there a lot of mining in this part of the country? I've noticed that you have a lot of supplies for mining."

"Yeah, there are some claims around. Not many big ones, just a few smaller ones."

"I don't mean to sound nosy, but it seems to me that you would have a hard time selling that stuff to a bunch of soldiers."

"I got more customers than just these soldiers, you know. I got people coming in from all over. You think a man can make a living selling to these dang soldiers?"

"No, I guess not. But I've been here three or four days now, and I haven't seen anybody but army men."

"I have civilians come by ever so often. And when they do, I'm ready with whatever they need."

The storekeeper finished with Tom's order and placed it on the counter.

"Will there be anything else, Lieutenant?"

"No, that should do it. How much do I owe you?"

"I'll have to figure it up. I'll tell you what—I'll figure it up and write it down."

"Thanks anyway, but I would prefer to pay cash for it."

"Cash is a mighty scarce thing around here, Lieutenant. Are you sure? I mean, with the trouble the army's having with their payroll, I thought maybe you'd want to hold on to what cash you have."

"Yes, I'm sure. I'll pay for the supplies now. Speaking of the payroll trouble we're having, aren't you a little worried about the people being able to pay you?"

"No, I ain't worried. I'll get what's owed me."

After a long pause—and what Tom took as a threat—he said, "One way or the other!"

Chapter 5

Tom was still thinking about that last comment made by the storekeeper when Mike walked into the mess tent.

"How's it going, Tom? Did you talk to the storekeeper?"

"Yeah, I talked to him, and it was pretty interesting."

The two men sat and ate their meals while Tom told Mike what happened at the store that day. When they got done eating and got ready to leave, Sergeant Gibson walked in.

"Lieutenant Rivers, can I talk to you?"

"Sure, Sergeant. Tom, I'll meet you over at the saloon as soon as I'm done talking with Sergeant Gibson."

"Sure thing, Mike."

"So, Sergeant, what's up?"

"Well, I was at the captain's tent, when Sal from over at the store came in. And he was really mad."

"Really? Do you happen to know what he was mad about?"

"No. But I heard something about him wanting his money by next week because he wanted to close up and move on."

"Thanks, Sergeant. If you hear anything else, let us know, will you?"

"Sure thing, Lieutenant."

Tom walked out of the mess hall and across the street to the saloon. When he entered the saloon, he looked around for Mike. Mike was sitting at the bar, talking to the bartender.

"So what's new around here? It seems mighty slow."

"You got that right. The captain came in here earlier and told everybody that there would be no more credit at the store or in here. He said that until we got the next full payroll in, no one can charge anything anymore."

"You don't say. You wouldn't happen to know what brought all this on, do you?"

"Yeah. This morning, the storekeeper said he wants his money from everyone by next week. I know the captain was some upset about that."

Tom had just come up to the bar and had overheard what the bartender had been telling Mike.

"You know, that sounds strange. I just talked to the storekeeper, and the way he sounded, he wasn't real worried about it."

"Well, mister, I don't know what you two talked about, but he told the captain that he wants his money by next week or he's going to shut down and pull his freight."

"You know, you're the second person to tell me that tonight. Well, thanks for the drinks. Mike, what you say you and I go and talk to the captain?"

On their way to the captain's tent, Mike couldn't help but think about what the storekeeper had said to the captain.

"Tom, it just doesn't make any sense. After what you said about the storekeeper, I just can't imagine him doing this."

"I know, Mike. Maybe after we talk to the captain, we will go see that storekeeper."

Mike and Tom were just getting to the captain's tent when they heard someone arguing inside.

"Sal, I don't understand. You know the problem we're having getting the payroll here."

"Captain, that's not my problem—that's the army's problem. I want my money, and I want it next week! If I don't get it, I'm pulling my freight!"

With that said, Sal left the tent, and Mike and Tom went inside to talk to the captain.

"Well, gentlemen, I guess you heard that. I just don't know what to do. If we don't get a payroll through soon, I'm afraid we are going to have to shut this fort down."

"Yeah, Captain, we heard. I guess it's time for us to quit playing army and go back to playing Texas Rangers."

Chapter 6

"I don't like it, boss. They got the Texas Rangers involved now."

Stone Jackson sat on his big cowhide chair. He was thinking about what had happened at the fort the day before. Sal didn't know it, but he wasn't the only informant from the fort that Stone Jackson had. Stone had already heard about the conversation that Sal and the captain had before Sal got here today. And now here was Sal with some cock-and-bull story of Texas Rangers.

"Now settle down, Sal. How can you be sure this guy is a ranger?"

"I ran into him about three years ago down at Fort Worth. He was picking up some prisoners to take to the State pen."

"He didn't recognize you, did he?"

"No, I don't think so."

Stone was thinking about how long it had taken him to get this setup working. He was sitting pretty good now, and he didn't want to see it end just yet. He had put too much of his life into this, and the best thing about it was that no one suspected anything. He had been outside of Fort Stanton for about five years now. His cattle business supplied the army post with beef, and he was doing a little mining on the side. The mining was good. That's why he started knocking off the stages with the payroll. He knew that with an army fort moving in, sooner or later, settlers would start coming in also. And he wasn't ready for them to move into his territory. When he found Sal at the store, he really had it made. It had worked really easy. Sal somehow knew when all the payroll shipments left and what routes they were taking. And the people he used understood that tno one was to be hurt, and the only thing they were to take was the army's payroll. Now this. Sal was getting nervous and wanted to shut everything down.

"Sal, just rest easy. I'll have someone take care of that ranger. You just go back and tell that captain that you have reconsidered, and you're not going to pull your freight."

On the way back to the fort, Sal was thinking about the conversation he and Stone had. It had all been so easy. He had made friends with Corporal Pearson, and in doing this, he found out when the payroll runs were and the routes that they were taking. With a little money and whiskey, Pearson was putty in his hands. Now he had this damn ranger poking around. The best thing he could do was pack up and get out fast. Sal had been around long enough to know that if they started talking to Corporal Pearson, he would surely turn him in. Sal made up his mind; he would tell the captain what Stone wanted him to. But he was also thinking that if they didn't get this ranger soon, he was going to leave the county fast!

The Mexican walked into Stone's house.
"You send for me, señor?"
"Yeah, I've got a job for you. I need someone taken care of quick."
"Sir, who is it, and where is he?"
"It's a Texas Ranger. He's out at Fort Stanton. When you get there, you look up the storekeeper. Tell him who you are and what you want. He'll show you the man."
"Si, señor. No worry. I take care of problem."
Now that Stone had this taken care of, he could concentrate on what to do about Sal.

Chapter 7

It was a hot, sticky day at the camp. Not many people were around. The Mexican smiled and turned the white stallion into the corral. Now to get to the store without being seen. He would find out later that getting there without being seen was not as easy as he thought.

As the Mexican crossed the street toward the store, Sergeant Gibson was coming out of his tent. He decided that he would find out where this man was going. The Mexican was heading to the store, so Sergeant Gibson went around to the back of the store and slipped into the storeroom and waited. The Mexican walked into the front of the store and saw Sal behind the counter.

"I see that Stone doesn't waste any time," Sal said. "I guess you're here to take care of our problem."

"Si. Señor Stone said you show me this man. You show him to me, and I take care of him for you."

"OK, follow me."

When Sal and the Mexican left the store, Sergeant Gibson left by the back door. Now this was interesting. Gibson had suspected that Sal was mixed up in this somehow. Now he had proof. First thing was to warn Mike and Tom and then see what the captain wanted to do about this.

Sergeant Gibson hurried over to the dispatch office to see if Mike and Tom were over there. Gibson entered the office, but there was no one around. He turned to leave when he heard someone coming.

"I don't know where they are, Captain. But as soon as I find them, I'll get them right over to your tent."

"Thank you, Corporal. I'll be waiting for them."

Corporal Jones entered the office and saw Sergeant Gibson standing there.

"Sergeant. I didn't know you were here. How can I help you?"

"Have you seen Lieutenant Rivers or Slade around?"

"You know, Sergeant, it's funny that you should mention them. The captain and I were just talking about Lieutenant Rivers and those dispatches that Corporal Pearson sent out. I can't find those dispatches anywhere."

"Come on, Corporal. We have to find Lieutenant Rivers. There's a guy here that was sent to kill him!"

Chapter 8

Sergeant Gibson and Corporal Jones were headed over to the saloon. Sergeant Gibson saw Sal and the Mexican headed toward the livery stable.

"James, you hightail it over to the saloon and get Tom and Mike and meet me at the stables."

Sergeant Gibson just got to the back of the stable when he heard the Mexican and Sal talking.

"You get him in the street, and I'll take care of him."

"OK, Mex, but you just make sure you shoot the right man."

"Si. I get the right man."

Sergeant Gibson stepped out behind them.

"Sal, you and that Mexican drop your guns, now!"

Corporal James entered the saloon and saw Mike and Tom talking to the captain.

"Excuse me, sir, but Sergeant Gibson wants you two at the stable now. Captain, you might want to come along."

As the four men left, Corporal Pearson ran out to his horse and headed toward Stone Jackson's ranch. Stone needed to know about this; and after he told Stone, he was leaving the country.

"Hi, Captain. Thought you might want to meet these two guys. Sal here is behind the whole thing. Him and Corporal Pearson and Stone Jackson. That dead Mexican there was sent to kill Mike, but he wasn't fast enough for this scattergun here. I'm sure that Sal will lay out the whole story for you. If you don't mind, I'd like to go with Mike and Tom to get Stone Jackson."

"Sure thing, Sergeant. Corporal Jones, take this man to the brig and see that this other one gets buried."

"Yes sir, Captain."

Corporal Pearson just got to Stone Jackson's house. When he got inside, he saw Stone sitting behind his desk.

"Boss, I want my cut of the holdups. I don't think that your Mexican got the job done. I want out and fast."

"Slow down, Pearson. What's up?"

As Pearson was telling Jackson what was happening at the fort, Stone was getting madder.

"To top it off, boss, Sergeant Gibson caught Sal and the Mexican in the stable. And when I was leaving the fort, I noticed that white stallion on the outskirts of the fort."

Why did all this have to happen now? Stone had been so careful, and now it was all falling apart.

"OK, Pearson. Let me get your money, and we will both leave. I have it in my safe here."

When Stone opened the safe, he grabbed his pistol that he always kept there. He turned around and shot Pearson in the gut. Now he was gone. Why should he split this money with anybody?

Mike, Tom, and Sergeant Gibson heard the shot as they rode into the ranch yard. Tom jumped off his horse and was the first one in the house.

"Drop it, Stone! It's over!"

Stone turned around and fired too quickly. The bullet hit the doorjamb beside Tom. Tom fired twice and Stone was dead.

Mike and Sergeant Gibson came into the room.

"I'll bet that all that money in that safe is your payroll, Sergeant."

"You're probably right, Tom. I guess we had better get it back to the fort. And we will send someone out to bury these guys. The drinks are on me tonight."

Mike and Tom looked at each other and smiled.

Mike said, "Sounds good. What about it, partner?"

"Well, what are we waiting for? Get that money, and let's head to the fort."

LOST

Chapter 1

It had been a month since Tom and Mike had worked on a case. The time off was nice, but Mike was getting restless and was ready to get back to work. This was the longest period that Mike and his partner had been apart in the fifteen years that they had been together. As Mike read the telegraph from Major Clark, he wondered what Tom was up to and what he thought about this case.

"Sam, I guess we had better head to Austin. Tom's waiting for us, and it is time to go to work."

Sam just looked up from the corner of the room and wagged his tail.

Tom was sitting behind his desk when he received the same telegraph that Mike had. As he read the telegraph, he was thinking about Mike and Sam. It was going to be good to get back together with those two.

"Mr. Slade, are we done here today? Because if we are, I'd sure like to hit that fishing hole."

That was Bobby Wright. Bobby was a fifteen-year-old boy that Tom had hired to clean his office and take care of his horse. Bobby and his sister had lost their parents about two years ago, and Tom knew that they could use the extra money that Bobby made around here. Tom looked up from his paperwork.

"Did you get everything done? Feed my horse, sweep the office?"

"Yes, sir. I gave your horse a good rubdown too."

"OK, Bobby, but you make sure you leave some fish in there for me."

"Ah, Mr. Slade, you know you don't never have no time for fishing."

"Yeah, but one of these days, I'm going to take you down there and show you how to fish. Now get out of here before I find something else for you to do."

As Bobby was leaving the office, Major Clark walked in.

"Hold on there, Bobby. Slow down a little."

"Yes, sir, but I got to get out to the fishing hole. There's a big catfish just waiting for me to catch him."

"OK, but if you catch him, you tell your sister that Tom and I expect to be invited over for a fish dinner."

"Yes, sir, I will."

"Well, Tom, I see you got my message. Mike should be here in about two or three days."

"Yes, sir, but I'm willing to bet you that Mike's already on the trail and will be here tomorrow night."

"Yeah, you're probably right. Mike isn't one to take a lot of time sitting around, is he?"

"OK, Major, now that we got the small talk out of the way, what is the next case all about?"

"I got the same message that you and Mike got. Like it said, this one is coming from the governor. You are supposed to meet him at the mansion Friday night, and he will fill you in then."

Mike and Sam had been on the trail for a day now. This was Tuesday, and he had to be at the governor's mansion by Friday. That was no problem. It sure would be good to get back to work.

Up on a mountain, a man was looking through his field glasses at Mike and Sam. A couple more yards and he would have him. Mike came around a bend in the trail, and he heard the boom of a rifle. As he was falling, all he could remember was the sound of the rifle.

The unseen marksman got up and mounted his horse. That was one who wasn't going to see the governor.

Chapter 2

Sam was sitting by Mike when the old man and his mule came out of the mountains.

"Well, Rosebud, looky what we got here. This fellow must've run into some unfriendlys. I guess the Christian thing to do is see if we can help this fellar."

As the old man got nearer, Sam started growling and pacing back and forth between the old man and Mike.

"Now you just take it easy, mutt. Rosebud and me just want to help this fellar."

Sam still stood his ground but finally let the old man near Mike.

"He ain't dead, Rosebud. He got him a wallop on his skull. We'll pack him back to the cabin."

After the old man caught Mike's horse, he got Mike on the saddle, tied his wrists to it, and headed off into the mountains.

"Well, mutt, he's going to make it."

They were in the cabin, and the old man was doing what he could to make Mike as comfortable as possible. Sam was lying by the fire when Mike started moaning.

"Well, I see you finally woke up. You been out for three days now."

Mike looked around. The cabin was small and untidy. There were two bunks—the one he was in and another on the other side of the room. He noted a potbellied stove in the center of the room and dirt floors.

"Where am I? Who are you?"

"You're in my cabin in the mountains. Rosebud and me found you and your mutt back down the trail about three days ago. You was shot and left for dead.

"Now, do you know anybody who would want you dead? I know it wasn't for money. I went through your pockets, and you only had about thirty dollars and no papers telling who you are."

Mike's head was throbbing, and his vision was blurred.

"No, I don't know who would shoot at me. I don't even know who I am."

It was Saturday morning, and Tom was sitting in his office. Mike hadn't showed up at the governor's mansion last night. That wasn't like Mike at all. Something must have happened—but what? The governor gave Tom the file on their next case. He would give Mike until tomorrow, and if he wasn't here by then, Tom would go hunting for him.

It was Monday morning, and Tom was at the stable, saddling his horse.

"Tom, I gave that case to someone else. You don't worry about it. You just find Mike and know what's happened to him."

"I will, Major. You tell Bobby to check for messages from me or from Mike, will you?"

"Sure thing, Tom. You be careful."

Tom knew where Mike was before he was supposed to meet him at the governor's mansion. So that would be where he started his search.

Chapter 3

Tom checked into the hotel at Tablerock. He asked the person behind the desk if he had seen Mike around.

"No, sir. He checked out about a week ago. Him and that dog of his."

"Thanks. I'll be around town for a while. If you hear anything, let me know will ya?"

"Sure thing. If you don't mind some help, why don't you try the gold strike? If anybody's seen him, you should hear it over there."

"Thanks. I think I will. But first, I'm going to get something to eat."

Tom found his way to the dining room and found a table.

"We have venison and buffalo. Which would you like?"

Tom looked at the man talking to him.

"Well, I don't know. Just give me whatever is ready and some coffee."

The man left and went to the kitchen. Tom looked around.

There were about eight people in the dining room. One person kept looking over at Tom. He finally got up and walked over to Tom's table.

"Heard you was looking for your partner."

"Yeah, that's right."

"My name's Jack Laurance. I'm the sheriff here in Tablerock."

"Nice to meet you, Sheriff. My name's Tom Slade, and I'm a Texas Ranger."

"Yeah, I figured as much. Mike gave a pretty good description of you."

"So you know Mike then?"

"Yeah, he was always at my office, just talking. He was pretty antsy. Ready to get back to work. As a matter of fact, he couldn't wait to start on the next case."

"So he told you about our case then?"

"No, he didn't tell me. But when he got that telegraph, he sure lit out of here fast."

"Do you know when he left? He was supposed to meet me in Austin last Friday, but he never showed up."

"Yeah, he left here last Monday. Said something about meeting you in Austin. He should have been there by Wednesday."

"Yeah, I know, and he never showed. Do you know what trail he took out of town?"

"I sure don't, Tom. But if you go to the livery stable and talk to the holster, he might be able to tell you."

"Thanks, Sheriff. I'll do that. And I'll poke around town some more if you don't mind."

"Fine with me. If you need any help, just call on me."

Tom finished his meal and left to go see the holster.

At least Tom knew Mike had been seen before he left. Leave it to Mike to strike up a friendship with the local law. That was just like him. Once a lawman, always a lawman.

Tom made his way across the dusty street to the stables. He took note of the buildings as he was walking. Tablerock was like most of the other towns that he had been to—a bank, a dry goods store, the sheriff's office, the hotel, a saloon, and five or six houses. He just couldn't understand why Mike chose this town to spend his vacation in.

Tom finally made it to the stables. He walked through the big doors at front. *They must have some freight wagons come through town,* he thought to himself. That would explain the big doors and the enormous width of the barn. They must pull the wagons in here and unload them. He had noticed the ropes and pulleys hanging from the rafters overhead.

While he was still looking around, he noticed that there were enough stables to hold two dozen horses.

"Can I help you, mister?"

Tom turned around and saw a middle-aged man, about five feet seven inches tall, with a walrus mustache stained by tobacco juice. He had friendly eyes.

"Yes, I sure hope you can. My name's Tom Slade. My partner was in your town about a week ago, and the sheriff said that he boarded his horse here."

"Could be. What did he look like?"

After Tom told the man what Mike looked like, the holster smiled.

"Yeah, I remember Mike. Right fine fellow. Ain't in trouble, is he?"

"I don't know, old-timer. He was supposed to meet me in Austin last Friday, and he didn't show. I was hoping that you knew when he left town and which way he went."

"Why don't you come into my office? I have coffee on, so we will have a cup, and I'll tell you what I can."

Chapter 4

Mike woke up in the middle of the night. The dog was still lying beside his bed. The old man was snoring away on the other cot across the room. His head still hurt. He was getting some strength back, but he still couldn't remember much of anything. He got up from the cot and walked to the front door of the cabin. The dog got up and followed him out onto the porch. Well, that was something. Even though he couldn't remember much, this dog seemed to think that they belonged together.

"I see you're up. You hungry? If you are, I can rustle us up some grub."

Mike turned around to find the old man behind him.

"Yeah, I guess I could do with some coffee. By the way, old man, how did I get here anyway?"

"I'll tell you what, son. You just come on back inside and sit down, and I'll tell you all that I know. By the way, my name is Orville—Orville Brandstone."

Mike and the man sat over coffee at the table.

"I guess it's been about a week now, son. Me and Rosebud was coming down Saunder's Peak, and we heard a shot. Well, mister, we just stayed where we was until I was sure whoever was doin' the shootin' was gone. Then me and Rosebud did some investigating, and we found you with a bullet crease along your skull. Yes, sir, and let me tell you—it took a powerful lot of convincing that dog that we meant you no harm."

"Well, Mr. Brandstone, I'm sure glad that you came along when you did. I'm sorry about that dog, but the way he acts, I guess that me and him are supposed to be together."

"You mean you don't know if that dog is yours or not?"

"No, sir, I sure don't. I can't even remember who I am."

"Well, son, I got your saddlebags over there in the corner. If you want, we can go through them and maybe shed some light on the subject."

"Yes, sir, I would sure like that. But I'm awfully tired now. It can wait until morning."

"OK, son. Whenever you're ready, you just let old Orville know."

Mike made it back to his cot and, within minutes, was sound asleep. Orville looked over at Mike sleeping and then over at the dog lying by the stove.

"Well, dog, I kinda like this fellow. And since he can't seem to help himself, it's up to me and you."

There was bright sunshine coming through the window when Mike woke up.

"Good morning. Coffee's on, so come on over here. I got some questions for you."

Mike got up from his bunk and went out and washed his face. Only when he came back inside did he notice that the saddlebags were on the table, and its contents were out.

"Well, son, I was going through these all night. I came up with three names. There are some dispatches in here, and in almost every one of them, the same name comes up. There is a Mike Rivers, a Tom Slade, and a Major Clark. All three of these people are Texas Rangers. I guess that you are one of them. Now we just have to figure out which one."

Chapter 5

Tom had learned a lot from his talk with the holster. He had learned what day, what time, and most importantly, which way Mike had gone when he left town. Tom was getting dressed when someone knocked on his door. Tom grabbed his pistol and opened the door slowly.

"Jack. Come on in. I was just getting dressed and heading down to get something to eat."

"That may have to wait, Tom. I need you to come over to the office. We found something of Mike's last night."

Tom finished dressing, and he and Jack left the room and headed over to the sheriff's office.

"Tom, here is Jason Long. He's a puncher from over in the hills. Jason, this is Tom Slade of the Texas Rangers. Tell him exactly what you told me."

"Well, it was like I was telling the sheriff here. Me and some other boys were rounding up cattle around Saunders Peak day before yesterday. We had found about thirty strays when we came up on this."

He pulled a Texas Ranger's badge out of his pocket and handed it to Tom.

"Can you show me exactly where you found this, Jason?"

"Yes, sir. There's one other thing. While we was nosing around, we found a place up on the hill where somebody had been lying, waiting. It looked like your friend has been shot."

Tom stood there with his mouth open. Finally, he asked, "Did you find the body?"

"No, sir, we surely didn't. And the dumbest thing is we couldn't find no trail either."

"Sheriff, I'm going to go look for Mike. Will you send a wire to Major Clark at Rangers headquarters for me and ask him to send a Sergeant Gibson?"

"Sure, I will, Tom. But if you need help, you have all you need here. We will help in any way that we can."

"Thanks, Jack. I'll need all the help I can get. But I need Sergeant Gibson to help me track. Aside from Mike, he's the best tracker I know. And since it's Mike I'm looking for, I need Sergeant Gibson."

"OK, Tom. But it's getting dark now. We'll send the message. And if Sergeant Gibson is as good as you say, why don't we just wait till he gets here, and all of us leave together. That should only be another day or so."

"OK, Jack, we'll wait. But in the meantime, I'm going to ask around town and see if anybody knows anything about this shooting."

When Tom left the sheriff's office and headed back to the hotel, the sheriff turned to Jason.

"Jason, you go send that message to Major Clark. When you get done, meet me over at the gold strike. You won't be punching cows for a while, so you are now my deputy. I didn't know Mike that well, but he was a straight shooter. And if anybody killed him, he will hang for it!"

Chapter 6

Sergeant Gibson had just arrived at Tablerock. He had been two days on the trail. When Major Clark called him into his office and read him the wire, he didn't know what to think. Rod Gibson was ex-army. He had known Mike and Tom for about two years now. They had been at Fort Stanton on a case when the three had met. He liked them both really well, and now they needed his help. Rod went to the hotel to find Tom. He walked up to the desk and looked at the registry. That was one good thing. Tom was still registered here.

"Well, Tom, at least you waited for me and didn't go off half-cocked like the major was afraid you would."

Rod went up to Tom's room, but he wasn't anywhere around. As he was coming back down the stairs, he saw Tom walk into the dining room. Rod walked over to Tom's table.

"Can a man get some decent coffee around here?"

"Rod! Glad you're here. You sure made good time."

"Well, you said Mike was in trouble, so here I am. What's going on anyway?"

As the two men ate, Tom filled Rod in on what he knew so far.

"So you see, Rod, the only thing that we really know is that someone took a shot at him. We haven't found a body, his horse, or that stupid dog of his."

"Well, Tom, if he's still alive, we will find him. Is there anyone else that can help us?"

"Yeah, there's the town sheriff and his deputy. They're over at the jail waiting for us right now."

When Tom and Rod arrived at the jail, the sheriff and Jason Long were waiting for them.

"Sheriff Laurance, I would like you to meet Sergeant Gibson, one of the best trackers I know."

"Nice to meet you, Sergeant. This is my deputy, Jason Long. He can take us right to the place he found Mike's badge. Then it's up to you, I guess."

"Nice to meet you both, but call me Rod. I'm no longer in the army. I'm just a regular citizen."

Chapter 7

Mike and the old man were mending some fences around the place. It was a warm, sunny day.

"What would you say we take a little breather, son? You can work an old man like me to death. There's one thing for sure—whoever you are, you ain't afraid of no work."

Mike put down his tools and walked over to the bench in front of the cabin and sat down.

"I sure wish I could remember something. I feel so useless like this. The only thing that we know for sure is that I have this day, and I'm supposed to be a Ranger."

"Well, son, it's only been a week since I found you. These things take time. You lost a lot of blood. Now I ain't no doctor, and maybe that doesn't have anything to do with it, but that might have something to do with your remembering or not. But you got to have time to get your strength back."

"I guess you're right, but I just wish I could remember something. I think I'll go back inside and read those letters again."

"Suit yourself, son. But take it easy, huh?"

Mike went back inside the cabin and sat down on his bunk. How many times had he been through those saddlebags? And still he couldn't remember anything. Once again, he read the letter dated three weeks ago.

You are to meet Tom in Austin. You will get your next assignment from the governor.

Major Clark

That meant that he was Mike Rivers. Well, he had a name, a dog, and he was a ranger. Now he just had to get it all to make sense. *Tom.* He couldn't remember anybody named Tom. Nor could he place a Major Clark. The more he thought, the more confused he became.

"Are you getting anywhere with that yet?"

It was the old man. He came in and sat down beside Mike.

"Well, I guess that since I was supposed to meet Tom in Austin, and the letter was signed by Major Clark, that makes me Mike Rivers. I do kinda remember one name—Sam—but I don't know who it is."

Out of the corner of his eye, the old man saw the dog's ears perk up at the name of Sam.

"Say that name again, son."

"What? Sam?"

With that, the dog came over and sat at Mike's feet.

"Well, son, now we know who Sam is. I think that sooner or later, the rest will come back to you."

"I sure hope you're right, old man. I sure hope you're right."

Chapter 8

It was sunny when the four men left Tablerock. Jason Long was in the lead.

"It should take us about an hour to get to Saunders Peak."

"Well, Jason, let's go. The quicker, the better. I know that Tom and Rod want to find out what happened to Mike."

The country the men were riding in was rough and slow-going. As they rounded the bend, Jason held them up.

"This is where I found the badge and up there," he said, pointing to some outcroppings of rock about 150 yards away, "is where someone had been waiting."

Tom and Rod looked around the spot where the badge had been found.

"Tom, there ain't much blood. Of course, the trail is old, but my guess is that he ain't dead. Hurt bad though."

"I think you're right, Rod. What do you think? You think somebody got him out of here and is helping him?"

"Well, Tom, you know that dog of his. If someone had tried, they would have had to get past him first."

"Yeah, you're right. But sometimes that dog will surprise you. I mean, if the person that found Mike was trying to help, that old dog just might let them."

"What are you getting at, Tom?"

"Well, let's look at it this way. If the person lived in these hills, chances are they don't want to be found. But that dog, he would have been worried about Mike. I've been around that dog for some time now, and I think that I can track him as good as I could track a horse."

"So what you're saying is this person spent a lot of energy trying to cover his trail, but he gave no thought as to what that dog was doing?"

"That's what I'm saying, Rod. Let's look for dog droppings and some of his hair. We find that and I'll bet you the first round when this is over that we find the dog and Mike."

"Well, Tom, I ain't never trailed a dog before. But I guess there's a first time for everything."

Tom and Rod rode back over to where Jason and the sheriff were waiting.

"Sheriff, you and Jason might as well head back to town. Rod and I can handle it from here."

"Sure thing, Tom. When you three get back, dinner is on me."

"Thank you, Sheriff. I'm sure that Mike would appreciate that."

As the sheriff and Jason turned back toward town, Rod looked at Tom.

"I don't believe I'm saying this, but let's track us a dog."

Chapter 9

Mike and the old man were sitting on the bench outside the cabin.

"How long have you lived up here, old man?"

"Going on thirty years now. Moved here right after my wife and son passed away."

Mike had a funny feeling. Something the old man said had triggered a memory. *Wife and son.* Mike had a wife and son. Did he still have a wife and son? No. They were dead. Not just dead—murdered. *Tom Slade.* That name. Now who was he? Partner. Tom Slade was his partner. They had met in Pine Ridge. Now he remembered! The Clayton Brothers had murdered his family, and Tom was at Pine Ridge. Tom put them in jail.

"Yes, they passed away from the fever. So's I just moved up here and been alone ever since."

"Do you want to hear about my life, old-timer?"

"Son, that's great! I durned straight I do."

So that's how it was when Tom and Rod rode up to the cabin. Mike and Sam were sitting with the old man. And Mike was just jabbering away.

"Now, don't that beat all, Tom. Here we are worried to death about this galoot, and here he is having himself a tea party."

"Now, Rod, don't be so hard on him. You know that sometimes he acts like he's a little touched in the head."

With that, Mike and the old man burst out laughing.

"What did I say?"

"Tom, you and Rod get on down from those horses. Have I got a story for you!"

FRIENDS IN NEED

Chapter 1

It had been about three years since Tom had heard from the Walkers. It would be good to see them again—or at least, Sarah. According to the message, Sarah had said that Able left for the Dakotas three months ago. The Walkers were a fine family that owned a ranch just west of Fort Worth. It wasn't a very big ranch, but it had always provided a good living.

Now Sarah didn't know what to do. Able had never been gone this long, and she had to let the hands go—all except Mark. He came to the West with the Walkers. He had been one of Able's oldest friends.

"Mark, I just don't know what to do. I mean we are out of cash. And if we don't get this beef to Dodge next month, I'll be forced to sell."

"Now, Mrs. Walker, just don't you worry about that. When Mike and Tom get here, we will make that drive."

"I sure hope you're right, Mark. I just wish I knew where Able was. I need him here."

"I know, ma'am. I wish he was here too."

Tom walked across the street to Major Clark's office.

"Good morning, Tom. Can I get you a cup of coffee?"

"Thanks, that sounds good."

After Tom was seated and had his coffee, he showed the telegram to Major Clark.

"I know that this isn't official business, Major, but it's kinda slow. So I was wondering if you would let Mike and me take some time off to help these people."

"I don't see why not, Tom. How long do you think you'll need?"

"Well, Major, we have to get them to Kansas. See, I was thinking about a month."

"Sure thing, Tom. Why don't you take Sergeant Gibson with you? He needs to get out and do some real work for a change."

"Thank you, Major. I think that's a good idea. He is getting kinda fat and lazy."

Tom left the major's office and took out across the compound. The first place that Tom stopped was at the store.

"Hi, Steve. Have you seen Mike or Sergeant Gibson?"

"No, Tom, I sure haven't. Have you tried the diner?"

"No, not yet. Thanks. If you see them, tell them I'm looking for them, will you?"

"Sure thing. If I see them, I'll tell them."

After Tom left the store, he walked over to the diner. He found a table and sat down to a cup of coffee and a meal.

"Mary, have you seen Mike and Sergeant Gibson?"

"Well, hello to you too. Come into my place. No 'good day' or nothing. All you want is to find those two no-goods."

That was Mary—always kidding. Tom knew she would know where the two were at. It was common knowledge that Gibson had been sparking Mary for the last month or so. And if anyone knew where Gibson was, it would be Mary.

"I'm sorry, Mary. How are you this morning?"

"Fine, thank you. If you want to find those two no-goods, they came in this morning for breakfast."

Now, Tom knew from experience with Mary that she took her own sweet time about everything. So while Tom was waiting for more news from Mary, he had another cup of coffee.

Mary was waiting on other tables and talking to some other ladies.

"Mary, how has it been going with you and Sergeant Gibson?"

"Really good, Susie. But Tom just came in asking for him and Mike, and you know what that means."

"You don't know that for sure, Mary."

"Yes I do, Susie. And believe you me, I don't intend to make it easy for Mr. Slade. If he wants them, he is just going to have to wait."

Well, it was time to get moving, and Tom knew that he would have to go to Mary and ask again. Tom got up and walked over to where Mary and the other ladies were sitting. Tom tipped his hat. "Ladies, how are you today? Do you mind if I talk to Mary for a minute?"

"That's fine with us, Mr. Slade. But she's already spoken for. Why don't you talk to me instead?"

With that said, the other women, including Mary, started laughing.

Tom was turning a little red. He could handle almost anything, but when it came to talking to women, he was just no good at it.

"Now, Susie! That's not very nice—to embarrass Mr. Slade like that. If he wants to talk to me, I think that the least I could do is listen."

"Thank you, Mary. If you know where Mike and Sergeant Gibson are, I sure would like for you to tell me."

"Well, Mr. Slade, like I said, they had breakfast here this morning and then said something about fishing."

"Thank you, Mary. I'll be seeing you."

As Tom left the diner, Mary called out, "Tom, you all be careful. And you tell that man of mine to stop by and say good-bye."

"Yes, ma'am, I surely will."

Tom found the two men at the river.

"Hey, you two. Catching anything?'

"Hi, Tom. Yeah, we got us a couple of nice ones right now. I just wish that Mike here could catch some."

"You old sidewinder. I could outfish you any day of the week."

"OK, you two, stop arguing. I got us a job for the next month. Let's get into town, and I'll tell you all about it. Oh, and Gibson, you make sure you go by and see Mary. I told her that you would. And I sure don't want her hunting me down because you didn't stop."

Chapter 2

Tom, Mike, and Gibson walked into the diner.

"I see you found them. I guess that you will be leaving for another job?"

"Come on, Mary. You know what line of work we are in."

"Yes I do, Rod. But you're not even a ranger. Why do you have to go?"

Mike and Tom had heard this argument before. True, Rod wasn't a ranger, but he sure was useful to them. He could track a snake over a flat rock; and besides that, he was the best cook.

"Come on, Mary. You know that those two can't make it without me. And besides, I'm getting kind of restless just sitting around here."

Tom decided that he would throw his friend a lifeline.

"Now, Mary, you know that if Rod ain't with us, Mike and I would probably starve to death—not to mention get lost."

"Tom Slade, don't tell me that. You two got along just fine before you met Rod. Now that he met me, you just want to take him away."

"Mary, you know better than that. But if we leave ole Rod here, you're liable to latch on to him and make an honest man out of him."

Mike couldn't help but laugh. And why not? Everyone else was too. Everyone but Rod Gibson.

"Hold on there now. Can't a man talk for himself around here?" Rod said.

Mike was still laughing. "Well, ole buddy, it's like Tom says—if we leave you here, you might end up hitched."

"Now, Mike, don't embarrass the old cuss. Besides, Mary here's got more sense than to want to tie up with an old buzzard like Rod."

Now Mary was feeling a little uncomfortable.

"Now listen here, you three. I'll see who I want. And as far as marriage, Rod hasn't even asked me yet."

"Now see that, Tom? If we leave old Rod here, she'll for sure have an apron on him by the time we get back."

"Now just wait a cotton-pickin' moment. Who said that I was going to get married? And what's this about me wearing a silly apron? You can bet your months' wages I ain't about to wear no apron!"

Mike was really enjoying this now. He really couldn't get under Tom's skin, but Rod was a different story.

"Come on, Tom. We don't need ole Rod anyways. I mean the work's going to be hard, driving those cattle and all."

"Yeah, you're probably right, Mike. We're better off without him. Anyway, all he would do is bellyache and pine away for Mary here."

Rod was listening to all this and getting madder by the minute.

"Are you sure that all you are going to do is move cattle?"

"That's all, Mary. We are going to Fort Worth to help some friends of mine."

"OK, Tom. But you promise to be careful and take care of those two. Especially Rod. Because when he gets back, whether he likes it or not, he's going to make an honest woman out of me."

"Yes, ma'am. You heard that, didn't you, Mike? Sounds like we are going to have a wedding when we get back."

"Yes, sir, I surely did. Don't you worry none about it, Mary. We will get him back safe and sound."

Chapter 3

The three men were on the trail to Fort Worth.

"According to Sarah's wire, Able has been gone for about three months. She said he went to Deadwood on some business, and they haven't seen or heard from him since."

"Well, Tom, I guess all that we can do is get her cattle to market. And maybe by the time we get back, they will have heard something about Able."

"I sure hope you're right, Mike. I guess she has only one hand left at the ranch. A guy by the name of Mark. Been with them for years now."

Rod was riding along, kind of dozing in the saddle, half-listening to the conversation and thinking of Mary.

"Do you know how many head she's got, Tom?"

"Yeah, Rod. Right in the wire, she said about eight hundred. She said that if she gets them sold, she will be able to pay the ranch off. But if we don't get them there by next month, she'll lose the ranch."

The three men kept riding toward Fort Worth.

They had put a hard day's ride in and were looking for a place to camp for the night. Mike had been scouting ahead when he came up on a camp.

"Hello, camp. I'm coming in with my hands empty."

"Come on in then."

Mike rode up to the camp, looking it over. He decided that he didn't like the looks of it all. The man who spoke first was big, unshaven, and had a little too much liquor in him.

"Hey, what's the meaning of that? I thought you said you were coming in with your hands empty?"

"Yeah, you must think I'm some kind of tinhorn, friend. I never ride up empty-handed." Mike looked around. There were six men here, and none of them looked like cowhands.

"Light and set, stranger. There's coffee and beans in the pot."

"Thanks, but I'm fine right here."

Mike's rifle was covering two of the men across the fire.

"Now, mister, that ain't very friendly. Why don't you put that rifle in the boot and get on off that horse."

The voice was behind Mike. He couldn't believe it. He had only counted six horses. But there were seven men. Mike slid his rifle in the boot and got off his horse.

"Now you just unbuckle that holster real easy and let it drop."

Mike dropped his guns and slowly turned around to see who was behind him.

"Now, mister, we mean you no harm. Just do what we say, and you'll live to see tomorrow. All we want is your horse. Mine stepped into a gopher hole and broke his leg. So what we are going to do is tie you up real tight and get on out of here."

Two men grabbed Mike's arms and dragged him over to a tree and tied him up.

"Now, mister, we're going to leave the fire going and ride out of here. Your two friends might find you, or they might not. Now, I know what you are thinking. You figure to wait for your friends, and when they get here, you'll send them after us. Well, you could do that, but you might want one of them to fix your leg for you."

With that said, one of the other men took out a club and hit Mike over the head. Before Mike passed out, he heard a shot and felt a sharp pain shoot through his right leg.

Chapter 4

"He's coming around, Tom."

Mike was waking up. His head was throbbing, as well as his leg.

"How are you feeling, partner? You were out for quite some time."

"I've felt better, Tom. Did you catch those guys?"

"No, we didn't. By the time we found you, they had a good two-hour start on us. What happened here anyway?"

While Mike was telling Tom what happened, Rod was scouting around to see which way the horse thieves went.

"I found their tracks. Looks like they're headed toward Fort Worth."

"Well, that's where we're headed. So if they stop there, we should run into them somewhere."

"Yeah, Tom. That sounds good. But how are we going to get Mike there?"

"We build a travois. We are only about twenty miles from the Circle W. He'll rest better there anyway. Sarah has a lot of experience with gunshot wounds."

After Tom and Rod built the travois, they loaded Mike onto it.

"You ready, partner?"

"Yeah, Tom. Let's go find those fellows. They'll be sorry if I get a hold of them."

"You just settle down, partner. We should be at the Circle W in a couple of hours."

The three men headed out—Tom in the lead, pulling Mike behind him, and Rod falling in behind.

The three men rode into the ranch yard about noon that day. Sarah came out of the cabin and onto the front porch.

"Tom, it's sure good to see you. I see you brought some friends with you. Mark, help them get this man into the house, will you please?"

When they had Mike comfortably in bed, Sarah, Tom, and Rod went into the kitchen.

"So, Sarah, tell us what's going on."

"Well, I don't know much more than I told you in the telegram. Able was supposed to be back weeks ago. He went to Deadwood to talk to the army about a contract for some beef."

"Why would he go all the way to Deadwood? Couldn't he have done it from here? I mean, they do have a telegraph office here."

"Yes, they do, Tom, but you know how Able was. He had been sitting around here all year. He was getting restless and wanted to hit the trail."

After they had eaten, Tom and Rod went out on the front porch to have a smoke.

"Tom, you know that with Mike laid up, it's going to be tough getting those cows to Dodge."

"He should only be laid up for a couple of days. Then we can hit the trail."

"There's still the matter of getting his horse back."

"Yeah, I was thinking of that too. What say we ride on into Fort Worth tonight and see if we can find those boys?"

"Mike, what I can't figure out is why drive them cattle all the way to Dodge? Why not sell them right here in Fort Worth?"

"I thought the same thing, so I asked Mark about it."

"Yeah? What did he say?"

"He said the market's better in Dodge. And before you ask, he said that they can't afford to ship them by rail."

"OK. Don't get so testy. I was just wondering."

Tom and Rod rode into town that night and went to the stable. They were looking for Mike's horse. It wasn't long before they found it.

"Well, Rod, there's the horse. Now we just have to find out where the riders are."

"You looking for the seven riders that came in with that horse?" a voice inquired.

Tom and Rod turned around to see the town sheriff.

"Yes, Sheriff. Especially the one that rode in on that chestnut."

The sheriff was a middle-aged man about five feet seven inches tall, overweight, and had a gray handlebar mustache.

"Well, I have them in the jail. They came in here about four hours ago, got drunk, and busted up the saloon. If you're here to bail them out, you can get them in the morning."

"No, sir. We don't want to bail them out. They stole that chestnut from our partner yesterday and shot him."

"Dead?"

"No, Sheriff, but they busted his leg. Now if you'll take us to see them, I'd like to talk to them."

"Sure thing. Follow me."

The three men walked down the street to the sheriff's office. When they got into the office, the sheriff stopped them.

"Now, I don't know who you boys are, and I'm generally a trusting kind of man—but before we go back there to see the prisoners, I'm going to need your hardware."

"Sheriff, I sure don't blame you one bit, and I don't do this for many men, but here you are."

With that said, Tom and Rod handed the sheriff their weapons. The sheriff led Tom and Rod back to the holding cells.

"Wake up! You boys have some visitors."

The seven men were in two different cells. They all looked up and rolled back over to go to sleep.

"You boys just rest easy. I'm going to ask the sheriff here to do you boys a big favor."

One of the men got up and came over to the iron bars.

"Yeah? And what might that be?"

"I'm going to ask him to keep you in here for at least a week. That should give me enough time to get my partner on the trail toward Kansas."

"Yeah? Why should we care about that?"

"Well, because he's the one that one of you guys shot and stole the horse from. Now that guy will hang. As for the rest of you, I just hope the sheriff takes my advice."

"Yeah? You don't scare us none. That feller ain't even here. By the time you get him back here, we will be long gone."

Tom just kind of smiled.

Then Rod broke in, "Should I tell this hombre, or should we let him find out on his own?"

"Tell me what?" The guy was a little worried now.

"Yeah, if you want to, go ahead," Tom said. "I mean, if I were in their boots, I'd sure want to know."

"Know what? Come on, guys, what's up?"

Rod looked at the guy and noticed that the other ones were paying attention also. The sheriff was leaning against the wall, as interested as the others. Finally, the sheriff spoke.

"You know what? I wouldn't tell them. I think I would just let all of them out in about two days. That should give your partner time to be back on his feet, shouldn't it?"

"Yeah. What do you think, Rod? Two days?"

"No, Sheriff. Give him three. That way, he will be so mad, we won't be able to stop him."

"OK. Three it is then."

The three men turned back toward the office. When they got to the door, one of the prisoners spoke.

"I ain't scared. They are just a bunch of talk."

Tom turned and looked at the one that had spoken.

"Yeah, you're right. We are a lot of talk. But I'm afraid that Mike Rivers doesn't talk as much as we do."

You could have heard a pin drop at the mention of the name.

"You telling me that horse belonged to Mike Rivers? The Texas Ranger?"

"That's what I'm telling you. I think I'd just cool my heels in here for about a week or so."

When the three got back into the sheriff's office and Tom and Rod were belting their guns on, the sheriff spoke, "Why didn't you tell me you were rangers? I would have never asked for your guns if I had known."

"That's all right, Sheriff. We aren't on official business anyway."

"Oh. Then what brings you to Fort Worth?"

"We just came to help a friend move some cattle. Do you know Able and Sarah Walker?"

"Yes, I do. And speaking of that, I have some bad news for Sarah. I got this telegram today. I was going to take it to her myself, but since you're going there, would you mind taking it?"

"No, Sheriff, I'd be glad to."

The sheriff handed the telegram to Tom. After Tom read it, he put it in his pocket.

"Thank you, Sheriff. I'll be sure to give it to her. And, Sheriff, do me a favor? Keep those guys in jail until we get out of town."

"Sure thing. You guys be careful. And tell Sarah I'm real sorry, will you?"

"I'll do that, Sheriff. And thank you again."

When Tom and Rod were in the saddle headed back to the ranch, Tom told Rod what the telegram said.

"Able was killed by a rockslide. The reason it took so long to get the message is that they had trouble identifying the body."

"That's rough, Tom. Now we got to get that herd through and sold for Sarah."

Chapter 5

Tom and Rod returned to the Circle W. The first thing they did when they got there was to show the telegram to Sarah.

"I thought something like this had happened. I guess after I sell the herd, I'll have to sell the place and move into town."

"Whatever you think is best, Sarah. How is Mike doing?"

"He's doing fine, Tom. He's out back helping Mark with a fence or something.

"Tom! What will I do about Mark? This has been his home for years. I can't just throw him out."

Tom was thinking about that when Mike and Mark walked in the house.

"Hey, I see you found my horse. Did you find that bunch of skunks that took him off me?"

"Yeah, Mike. They are all in the jail in town. When we ride out tomorrow, the sheriff wants you to stop in and point out the one who stole it from you."

While Tom, Mike, and Rod were talking, Sarah pulled Mark off to one side.

"Mark, I just received this telegram today. Able is dead."

"I'm sorry, ma'am. But I kind of figured something like that had happened."

"Yes, Mark, so did I. After you men finish this drive, I'm afraid I'm going to have to sell the ranch."

"I'm sure sorry to hear you say that, ma'am. But I can understand you wanting to. It sure ain't no life for a woman alone."

"No, Mark, it's not. But I want you to have first chance at buying the ranch."

"I appreciate that, ma'am. I really do. But I'm almost seventy years old. Too durned old to put roots down now. I guess when the drive's over, I'll just pull my freight and be on my way. Thank you just the same."

Sarah and Mark went back over to where the others were.

"Sarah, have you told Mark what you plan on doing?"

"Yes, Tom, I gave him first chance at the place, but he turned me down."

Rod was sitting, listening to the conversation.

"Mrs. Walker, you don't know me from Adam, but these boys know me pretty well. Ma'am, I have a girl back in Austin that's just chompin' at the bit to get married and settle down. And I guess I am too. So what I'd like to do is make you an offer on this place."

Mike and Tom looked at each other in amazement.

"Why, you old sidewinder. We was just funnin' back in Austin."

"I know you were, Mike, but I don't think that Mary was. And she is a durned sight prettier than either one of you."

"Mr. Gibson, I don't know what to say but thank you. You make that drive to Kansas, and I'll wire your girl for you. When you get back, we will have us the biggest wedding this town has ever seen."

"Thank you, Mrs. Walker. And, Mark, I would be right proud to have you stay on with Mary and me."

The next morning, the four men started the cattle on the trail to Dodge.

"What do you know, Mike. Ole Rod is really going to settle down."

"I never thought I'd see the day. But he sure got himself a good woman and a nice ranch."

"Yeah, Tom, he sure did!"

Harris County Public Library
Houston, Texas

Printed in the United States
By Bookmasters